DATE DUE

JAN 04 2016	
	PRINTED IN U.S.A.

Where I Belong

TARA WHITE

VANCOUVER   LONDON

Published in Canada in 2014
Published in the USA and the UK in 2015

Text © 2014 by Tara White
Cover illustration © 2014 by Julie Flett
Cover design by Elisa Gutiérrez
Book design by Jacqueline Wang

Mixed Sources

Cert no. SW-COC-001271
© 1996 FSC

FSC

Inside pages printed on FSC certified paper using vegetable-based inks.

Printed in Canada by Sunrise Printing, Vancouver, BC

2 4 6 8 10 9 7 5 3 1

Cataloguing-in-Publication Data for this book
is available from The British Library.

Library and Archives Canada Cataloguing in Publication

White, Tara, 1974-, author
    Where I belong / Tara White.

ISBN 978-1-896580-77-7 (pbk.)

    I. Title.

PS8645.H547W44 2014   jC813'.6   C2014-904500-X

The publisher wishes to thank
Jessica Denny, Alice Fleerackers, Meagan Hall, Ria Nishikawara,
Deirdre Salisbury, Shed Simas, Verity Stone and Hannah van Dijk
for their editorial help with the book.

Tradewind Books thanks the Governments of Canada and British Columbia for
the financial support they have extended through the Canada Book Fund, Livres
Canada Books, the Canada Council for the Arts, the British Columbia Arts
Council and the British Columbia Book Publishing Tax Credit program.

 Canada Council
for the Arts
Conseil des Arts
du Canada

 BRITISH COLUMBIA
ARTS COUNCIL
Supported by the Province of British Columbia

 Canadä

 LIVRES CANADA BOOKS

For Kevin and Celina.

I would like to thank everyone who helped me edit this story, in particular, Laura Fauman, Deirdre Salisbury and John Kieran Kealy.

I also wish to thank Canada Council for the Arts for the grant I received to write the first draft of this book.

—TW

Introduction

I ALWAYS KNEW I WAS ADOPTED. I NEVER THOUGHT TOO much about it. As the only black-haired, dark-skinned girl in town, I was used to feeling different. But everything changed after I met *him*.

Chapter 1

SNOWFLAKES SWIRLED THROUGH THE TREES, AND THE SKY was radiant, the way it always was when so much snow fell. It was almost the end of May, and I was happy for the freak snowstorm.

I was trudging through the woods, stopping from time to time to catch my breath, exhaling icy fog. The air was bitter cold. The snow stuck to my boots, making them feel like twenty-pound weights. I ducked often to avoid the low-hanging branches.

"Wait up, Carrie," Dana shouted as she pushed her way through the deep snow. "It's freezing out here. I'm exhausted."

I stopped in a clearing just short of a frozen creek and fell backward, arms outstretched to make a snow angel. I closed my eyes and felt the energy from the forest fill my body. The world stood still, as it always did when I was in the woods.

"Talk to me, Carrie," Dana said, coming up beside me. "What's going on?"

I sat up and studied her. She looked worried. Dana was my neighbour and best friend in the world. She knew all about my dreams. The wind blew icy crystals of snow into our faces. Little icicles dangled from her blonde bangs.

"I'm having those dreams again, Dana. I'm scared."

"You've always had dreams, Carrie. Why are you scared now?"

"They're different now. They're so real. There's a man with a gun."

"And what happens?"

"He's going to hurt someone."

"Who?"

I closed my eyes, afraid of my answer. "Me," I whispered.

Chapter 2

I am in the middle of a large crowd, trying to push my way forward. I'm confused and starting to panic. I don't know where I am or what I'm doing. I see a guy about twenty feet ahead of me. He's a teenager about my age with a long black braid. A white bird is sitting on his shoulder, staring at me. I am following him, even though he's a stranger. I'm connected to him by an invisible string. Each time he steps forward I feel a tug, and my body moves forward too.

I shout at him to wait, but my voice is drowned out by cheers from the crowd. The cheers slowly change into rhythmic drumming, and the stranger disappears into the sea of people.

"Carrie!"

He's calling me, I realize. I twirl around, scanning the crowd as I push my way through. I can't find him.

"Carrie, wake up!"

I sat up in bed, shivering.

"Carrie, we're late!"

It was Dana, shouting at me from the landing.

"C'mon, get up!" Dana shouted again. "My mom's waiting."

"Coming!" I shouted back. "Give me a minute to brush my teeth."

I met Dana at the bottom of the stairs.

"Hurry up, we have to meet Josh," she said. Her green eyes got all funny looking, like they always did when she talked about Josh. "He's bringing a couple of buddies with him. Hey, maybe you'll like one of them, and we can double-date."

"Yeah, right," I said, "hell will have to freeze over before my parents let me go on a date."

Mom came out of the kitchen. "Where are you girls off to?" She was wearing her little PJ set—pink tank top and short shorts. Her blonde hair was sticking out all over the place like she'd been electrocuted.

"Dana's mom is driving us to the Lanark Arena to watch the regionals." Not much happened in my hometown of McDonalds Corners, so a hockey tournament was a pretty big deal.

I grabbed Dana's wrist and pulled her toward the door.

Mom followed us down the hallway. "You need to study for your math final."

"My exam's not for another few weeks," I said.

Dad came out of the kitchen wearing only boxers. He was carrying a book in his hand, saving his place with a finger. He put his arm around Mom's shoulder.

"Come on," I said, staring at my half-naked parents, "would you two put on some clothes; we have company here."

They ignored me. As usual.

"You didn't say anything about going out," Mom said.

"It's the hockey tournament. Everyone's going."

"There are teams coming in from all over," Dana said. "It's going to be so cool."

"We don't think you should go," Dad said, looking over at Mom.

"What's the big deal anyway?" I grumbled. "It's just hockey."

"Fine," Mom said, rubbing her temples like I was giving her a migraine. "Your father and I will pick you up at five o'clock."

"But I'm getting a ride there and back with Dana."

"Your mother and I will be there to pick you up at five," said Dad, looking at me through the corner of his eye. "You can drive the car home. You need the practice. And put on your hat and gloves."

"Remember, the McDonalds Corners annual family fun day is tomorrow," Mom said. "And we'll be there all day, so you need to study tonight."

"You can never be too prepared for your exams," Dad piped in.

"Oh fine," I said, grabbing my hat and gloves from the box next to the door.

"What was that about?" Dana asked as we stepped into the car.

"I'm not kidding. Mom and Dad want me to become a nun. A doctor-nun."

Dana and her mom chatted the whole way there. I was jealous. I didn't have that kind of relationship with my mom. *We are just so different.* It wasn't just that I looked completely different from my parents. It was that we were different in every possible way.

DANA'S mom dropped us at the rink, and we stood outside to wait for Josh and his friends.

"I dreamt about the white bird again last night," I told Dana.

"Really?" she asked. She rubbed her hands together and breathed into them. "It's freezing out here."

"You should have brought a hat and gloves," I said, looking at her worn sneakers with a hole in the right shoe. "And boots."

"Thanks, *Mom*," Dana said. "I don't want to have hat-head, or look like a snowman in fuzzy winter boots."

I pulled off my hat and ran my fingers through my long hair.

"I never remember my dreams," Dana said.

"The white bird was sitting on some guy's shoulder, and it was watching me."

"The guy with the gun?"

"No, this guy was different. There was something about him—I was following him."

"Weird." She shrugged. "But, hey, all your dreams are very weird." Dana looked around the parking lot nervously, bouncing up and down to stay warm. "What's taking them so long?"

Just then a bus pulled up and a pile of boys stormed out, carrying hockey gear and joking around. Dana waved her hand in front of my face. "Earth to Carrie."

I was riveted by one of them. He was tall and wore a bomber-style, black and yellow jacket with a black hoodie underneath. He had a ball cap on backward, emblazoned with the number 19.

He looked right at me and smiled. I smiled back.

"Do you know that guy?" Dana asked.

"No, I . . . I don't think so," I stammered. "But maybe, I . . . I'm not sure."

"You're not making any sense."

"Look at them, Dana," I said. "They could be my brothers."

"What do you mean?"

"They have my black hair and my brown skin. All of them."

A horn honked, and Dana grabbed my arm. "Josh is here," she said, pulling me along. She introduced me to Josh's two teammates, Darren and Troy. But my mind was still on the tall guy from the bus. I felt like I knew him. I turned back to look for him, but his team had already disappeared inside.

We headed into the arena and sat down in the stands. Dana cuddled next to Josh, leaving me awkwardly wedged between Darren and Troy.

AFTER suffering through a couple of boring games, I needed a break.

"Be right back," I said, jumping up.

In the hallway, doors suddenly burst open and a bunch of guys barged in, carrying hockey bags and sticks. They laughed as they punched and jabbed each other. Then the tall guy from the bus stopped right in front of me.

He dropped his bag and smiled. "Hey, you're the girl from the parking lot, right?"

He had the most perfect skin, silky and chocolate brown. He had strong, high cheekbones and a square jaw. His long black hair was tied back in a braid. His black ball cap was turned the right way now. It had a small white bird stitched on its side.

The guy from my dream! I thought.

"What rez you from?" the boy asked.

"Me?" I mumbled.

"Yeah, you," he said, sticking out his hand. "I'm Tommy."

I reached out to shake it. His touch shot a shiver up my arm, then down my spine. I caught a giggle before it escaped.

"Carrie."

"So, what rez you from?" he asked again.

"Rez?" I mumbled.

"Yeah, rez. Reserve," he said, laughing.

I looked at him blankly.

"Indian reservation. You're Native, right?"

"Um . . . maybe, but . . . I don't know for sure. I was adopted," I stammered. "I live in McDonalds Corners."

"I'm from Akwesasne. It's a Mohawk reserve near Cornwall," he continued, still holding on to my hand. "You look familiar." He pulled me close and stared into my eyes. He had little gold flecks scattered in his dark-brown eyes. "I feel like I know you from somewhere."

My heart pounded and my knees felt shaky. I tried to take my hand away, but he tightened his grip. It felt strange to be standing next to someone with features so similar to my own.

"There you are! Josh's game is about to start." Dana came running up to us. "Oh," she said when she saw Tommy.

"Dana, this is Tommy," I said. "Tommy, this is my best friend, Dana."

"Hi," they both said in unison.

"Well," he said, finally letting go of my hand, "I've gotta go. We're playing next. I'm number nineteen. Watch me. Maybe I'll see ya after the game." He grabbed his bag, hiked it over his shoulder, winked and dashed off.

My cheeks felt like they were on fire.

"So," Dana said, grinning, "what's up with that Tommy guy?"

"Nn . . . nothing," I stammered.

"Nothing? Oh yeah!"

"Well, he thought he knew me." I hesitated. "Dana, I think he was the guy I dreamt about last night."

"Wow, that's so romantic," she gushed. "You're lucky. He's hot!"

"Maybe it's not him."

"It's got to be him. Definitely it's him. I like him."

"I had a funny feeling when I met him."

She laughed. "Like love at first sight?"

I felt the heat rise to my cheeks. "Not exactly. But a strong connection."

"It's love. It absolutely has to be love," she gushed, without a moment's hesitation.

BACK in the stands, Dana and I watched the match. Josh and his friends were playing against Tommy's team. I found his number right away. His team wore black and yellow jerseys and yellow socks. They made me think of giant bumblebees. Josh's team wore green and white. I followed Tommy as he flew across the ice. In what seemed like no time at all, the game was over.

"MOM and Dad will be here any minute. I'd better go out to the parking lot to wait for them."

"Want me to come?" Dana asked.

"No, that's okay. See you tomorrow."

"Okay, see ya."

I walked out of the stands and noticed a tall guy, surrounded by girls, about twenty feet away. *Tommy?* The guy turned and said something to a pretty girl standing beside him.

My heart sank.

I spun around and nearly bumped right into someone. "Oops, sorry," I said.

Looking up I saw that it was Tommy. My face was inches away from his chest. He smelled so good. I felt light-headed.

He leaned down, placed his lips next to my ear and whispered, "I know you. I just can't figure out how. Were you going to leave without even saying goodbye?"

"Well . . . ah . . . I thought you were busy over there." I pointed across the parking lot. "I thought that guy was you."

"That's my little brother, Adam. Everyone thinks we're twins," he said, placing a hand on my shoulder.

The touch of his hand sent electrical sparks shooting through me. My heart flip-flopped around in my chest.

"So, what'd you think of the game?"

"Um, good."

"Tommy, let's go!" someone shouted.

Tommy turned and held up a finger. "We're gonna go get a bite to eat," he said, turning back to me. "Wanna come hang with us?"

"Carrie." Mom and Dad were standing next to the car, waving.

"Kill me now," I said, waving back. "That's my parents coming to pick me up like I'm five years old. Sorry, gotta run." I turned toward them.

"Hold on," he said.

I stopped and stepped back, feeling a pull just like in my dream. I couldn't fight it.

"Until we meet again." He winked, tucked a note into my jacket pocket and turned to join his friends.

I watched until he disappeared around a corner.

"Carrie!" Mom shouted, again.

I turned again and started toward them.

Left, right, left, right. I commanded my feet. It took every ounce of self-control to not turn back and follow Tommy.

When I got over to Mom and Dad, they gave me a look that could melt steel.

Dad handed me the car keys, and I unlocked the driver's door, slipped inside and tucked myself in behind the wheel. Dad slammed the door shut.

"Who was that boy you were talking to?" Mom asked.

She climbed into the passenger seat beside me.

I reached over and unlocked the back seat car door. "What boy?" I asked.

"That boy you were with just now," Dad said, as he opened the door and sat down in the back.

"Just a guy."

"Did he ask you out on a date?" Mom asked.

I started up, pulled out of the parking lot and turned left on County Road.

"Well?" Mom persisted.

I forced a laugh. "No, he didn't ask me out."

"Well, he looks too old for you," Dad said from the back.

"He did ask what reserve I was from."

"Reserve?" Mom asked.

"Slow down, Carrie," Dad said. "You're driving too fast."

"Indian reservation," I clarified, easing up on the gas and pulling over to let a car pass.

"Honey, you're from McDonalds Corners," Mom said.

"I think he could be right," I mused.

"Right? Nobody knows where you're from," Mom said, shaking her head. "And what does it matter?"

"Boys are the last thing you should be thinking about," Dad added. "Watch the road, Carrie."

"Oh, I almost forgot to tell you," Mom said. "Science camp starts first Monday after school ends."

"Not another stupid summer school!" I shouted, speeding up to catch a green light.

"It's not summer school, it's a camp, honey."

"Yeah, right. No camp I've ever heard of gives you homework." I squeezed the steering wheel.

"We're really worried about your math and science grades, Carrie," Dad said. "You've got to get your grades up."

"But I got A's in English and history!" I bristled.

"Yes, and that's great, but you didn't do so well in math and science," Mom said.

"I don't need A's in every subject," I argued, overtaking a red minibus.

"Carrie, you'll never pass your driving test unless you keep to the speed limit," Mom said.

I slowed down. "Not everything in life is about science and numbers."

"You need math and science," Dad said, "to be a doctor."

"Just because both of you are doctors doesn't mean that I'm going to be one too."

"Carrie," Dad said in a firm voice, "you are going to science camp this summer. That's final."

"And there will be no time to get involved with boys," Mom added.

I felt a knot grow in the pit of my stomach, and I burned in silence for the rest of the ride. The feeling that I didn't belong in this family was getting stronger by the minute.

Chapter 3

*A man stands atop a pile of tires and
raises his rifle. I hear loud drumming. He
wears a bandana covering his mouth. He's
staring at me. His eyes look familiar.*

*I move toward him. His rifle is poised
to shoot. Suddenly I hear gunfire, and
crumple to the ground. My lower body is
on fire. The pain is excruciating.*

*A flash of white arcs across the sky
behind the man. He raises his rifle
again, bobbing his head in rhythm to the
drumming.*

I SHUDDERED, OPENING MY EYES.

Another one of those dreams, I thought.

I pulled the blanket up around my neck and looked
around. I felt safe in my bedroom. I had everything I could
possibly want here. *Why doesn't it feel like enough?*

I closed my eyes and took a deep breath, but the image of
the man in the bandana wouldn't go away.

I pulled my dream journal out of the nightstand and wrote everything down. *Who was that man, and why was he going to hurt me?*

I've had these kinds of dreams all my life. And sometimes my dreams even came true. *It's like I am some kind of freakish fortune teller or something.*

The first time I realized a dream of mine could come true was a couple of years ago. I dreamt about Mrs. Glenn, our neighbour, being pulled lifeless out of a burning car wreck. At dinner that night my parents told me Mrs. Glenn had been killed in an accident on the Trans-Canada. Dana was the only person I ever told about that dream. After that I started my dream journal.

I flipped through the pages of my dream journal.

September 25, 1989

Lights flashed and sirens blared. People screamed. I saw a woman with black hair sprawled in front of a car, in a pool of blood. From the back seat of the car came the tiniest little cries, barely audible.

That woman has been in my dreams for as long as I can remember. Every time I have this dream about her dying, I wake up crying.

November 1, 1989

I dreamt I was a kid with two long black braids and a brown mole on my right arm. I was banging and banging on a drum. There was a man banging his own drum beside me. I felt peaceful, happy.

Funny, I don't have any moles on my arm. This drumming sound is important. I know it. It's always there in my dreams.

December 3, 1989

I had the strangest dream last night. Someone wearing a black baseball cap and a bandana was staring at me. I heard drumbeats again. He held a gun dangling at his side, his finger on the trigger.

January 15, 1990

I was digging through our attic, looking for something I had lost, but I didn't know what. I lifted the lid of an old chest and pulled out a jewel-encrusted mirror. I peered into it. I could see the room behind me, but not my face. There was that drumming sound again.

Who am I really, I wonder?

January 31, 1990

Same dream about the person with the bandana. A fireball flew through the air behind him and set him ablaze. A white bird fluttered around him. He screamed. Same drumming sound.

March 10, 1990

A man was walking on a tightrope across the sky, directly in front of the sun. I stared at him and the sun blinded me. The drumbeat started and the man swayed on the tightrope like he was dancing.

Wow! That was a beautiful dream!

March 29, 1990

I was walking through the forest behind my house. It was so dark I couldn't even see the trees. I was lost, unsure of where I was going. I was about to call for help when I noticed a tiny light far in the distance. When I got close enough, I saw it was a white bird the size of an eagle. It was the most beautiful bird I'd ever seen. Every time I stepped toward it, it flew up and settled on a branch farther away. I followed it all the way to the edge of the forest. I felt peaceful. The drum beat quietly in the background.

That bird again. So cool.

April 3, 1990

I dreamt about the man in the bandana again. A shot rang out. I looked down. My feet were in a pool of blood. The blood vibrated with each beat of the drum.

April 15, 1990

The same man in a bandana again. This time there were people all around us, shouting. The man raised a gun above his head. The white bird fluttered around him. I stood frozen, watching as a ball of fire flew through the air and hit him in the back. He fired his gun, and other shots rang out. The sound of the guns turned into drumbeats, the same drumbeats. I looked down. The white bird lay dead at my feet.

This is so scary. I have to talk to Dana about this.

"CARRIE, come down for breakfast."

"Coming, Mom," I shouted, tucking my journal under my mattress. I tried to put the dreams out of my mind.

WHEN I got downstairs, the TV was blaring in the living room. A reporter was droning on about some protest, something about a Mohawk reserve and a golf course.

At breakfast Mom put her arm on my shoulder. "You're not eating, Carrie. Is something bothering you?"

"I've been thinking. Every family in McDonalds Corners fits together. But ours is different. I feel like I'm missing something, like I don't belong."

"Carrie, our family fits together," Mom said. "We all love each other."

Dad kept his face buried in the morning paper.

"I started wondering about all this stuff at the big family fun day picnic last weekend."

"What stuff?"

"Like where I belong. I never really thought about it before. But after seeing those hockey players, it made me think."

"You belong here with us, and we fit together just perfectly."

"Take Natalie's family. Her mom's an artist, and both Natalie and her little brother always win the art contests at school. Or Mark, his mom's an accountant, and Mark gets the highest grades in math class. Then there's Brian—he's a total jock, and both his parents were in the Olympics."

"So?"

"So I need to know something about my birth family.

I look so much like those boys on that hockey team. Maybe I'm Native, like them."

"We told you already, Carrie, when we adopted you the social worker didn't have any information about that," Mom said. "Besides, it's not important where you come from. You're our daughter and we love you."

"But I dream over and over about a woman with dark hair. Maybe she's my birth mother."

"I told you a million times that dreams don't mean anything," Dad said.

"My dreams do mean something," I argued, grabbing my plate and dropping it in the sink.

"Boys! That's what's making you crazy," Mom said, placing her plate in the sink. "You need to stop thinking about boys."

"And you have your exams to concentrate on," Dad added. "You have your future to think about." He shovelled a forkful of eggs into his mouth.

"This isn't just about me wanting to hang out with boys," I argued. "I look so much like those hockey players."

"Just promise us," Dad said, "that you won't be hanging around with that boy."

"He's too old for you," Mom piped in.

"Oh, fine," I said. *It's not like I'll ever see him again, anyway.* I turned around and stomped out.

"We love you, honey!" Mom shouted after me.

"Whatever," I mumbled, racing up the stairs. I pulled my drawers open and slammed them shut again. *They never listen to me!*

I suddenly remembered something important. *Tommy's note.* I ran downstairs, two steps at a time.

I rummaged through the hall closet looking for my jacket.

Mom was talking on the phone. "Thanks for getting the lab results back to me so quickly. A cut that doesn't heal, frequent urination, excessive thirst, blurry vision and fatigue—diabetes."

Diseases, drugs, tests. So boring. I raced back to my room with the note.

After quietly closing the door behind me, I pulled out the crumpled paper, opened it up and smoothed out the wrinkles. I held my breath for a moment. *Tommy's number.*

Chapter 4

*I'm a little kid, unsteady on my feet. I'm
walking through a maze, holding on to a vine-
covered wall. The woman with long dark hair is
watching me from a distance. I can't see her face
clearly. She's holding a small drum, and tapping
it with a stick. The sound echoes through the
maze. Her lips move like she is singing, but I
am too far away to hear her words.*

I HAD DOZED OFF IN DANA'S BACKYARD. WE WERE
stretched out trying to get a tan. It was crazy how fast the
weather had changed in just a couple of weeks. All the snow
had melted away.

I looked over at Dana. "I had one of those dreams again.
It was a good dream this time."

"Here, put some of this on," Dana said, tossing me a bottle
of sunscreen.

"I don't burn," I argued.

"Doesn't matter," she said.

Dana's whole family turned beet red in the sun, and she constantly slathered herself in sunscreen. I squeezed some into my hand and slopped it on my arms and legs.

"Do you remember that time when my mom got so burnt?" I said, laughing.

"Vaguely," Dana answered. "Was that the same time she dyed her hair black?"

"Yeah," I sighed. "She was trying to make herself look like me."

"Is everything okay? You've gone all moody again. What's up?"

"I know Mom and Dad love me, but they drive me crazy. They don't know who I really am. They wish I was just like them. And now they're freaking out about who I hang out with."

"Like me?" Dana asked. Her nostrils flared.

"No. It's Tommy," I said. "They don't like him. But it's not just Tommy. It would be the same with any boy."

"I knew it!" she shrieked. "You're in love with Tommy. You've been daydreaming about him, haven't you?"

"He gave me his phone number." I reached into my backpack and pulled out the piece of paper that was tucked away there.

"Are you going to call him?"

"I want to, but I don't know what to say."

"You could start with hello."

"Then what?"

"How are you? Where do you live?" Dana laughed. "Where do you go to school? Why do you visit me in my dreams?"

I threw a handful of grass at her.

"He visits you in your dreams, and he says he knows you from somewhere. Aren't you at all curious?"

"Yes . . . but . . ."

"Chicken," Dana squawked.

"Am not."

"Bwuck, bwuck!" She flapped her elbows.

I threw an ice cube at her. "I have an idea. You phone him and pretend to be me."

She laughed again. "No way." Then she stood up and dragged me off the chaise longue into the kitchen, handing me the phone.

"I wish I were like you," I whined. "You never have to struggle for something to say to anyone, not even a cute guy."

"Don't be a baby. You're way cooler than me. Now stop stalling."

I could feel my heart race. I was dizzy. My mouth felt pasty and dry.

I dialled. The phone rang and rang.

Just as I was about to hang up someone answered. "Hello?" a deep voice boomed.

I recognized it immediately. "Is this Tommy?"

"Yeah."

"Hi, Tommy," I said. "It's Carrie."

"I'm going to the school library before class," I told Dana on Friday morning on the bus. "Wanna come?"

"The library's boring," Dana complained. "All I do is carry stacks of books for you."

"I'm going to see what I can find out about Indian reservations," I said in a singsong voice, knowing that would get her interested.

"I'm in," she said.

The bus made one last stop and picked up the sisters, Aleisha and Samantha. They climbed in and sat in the seat in front of us.

Dana tapped Aleisha on the shoulder. "How did the competition go?"

Both girls turned around. "Aleisha placed first in dressage in intermediate," Samantha said shyly, "and I came in first in jumping."

"Way to go!" Dana and I said together.

THIRTY minutes later the bus dropped us off at school, and we headed inside.

"Good morning, ladies." Ms. Cook, the librarian, waved from behind her desk. She lifted her glasses to her eyes and pointed to a pile of books. "Carrie, I pulled out some books for you. I know how much you like V.C. Andrews, and her newest book just arrived."

Dana nudged me in the ribs and gave me a squinty-eyed look.

"Ah . . . not today, Ms. Cook. Thanks," I said, nudging Dana back.

"Can I help you find something else?"

"I need to look up some information on, um, Indians . . . Indian reservations. Mohawk Indian reservations."

She raised an eyebrow. "Oh?"

"I . . . um . . . have a history paper to research," I lied. I could feel my cheeks getting warm, and I knew they were turning red.

"A research paper at the end of term?"

"Yeah, one final paper."

Ms. Cook smiled, typed something on her computer and got up from her desk. Her long flower-print dress flowed around her ankles.

We followed her like she was the Pied Piper, as she looped through aisles of books. Finally, she stopped abruptly, and I bumped into her.

"Oops, sorry," I said, backing up against Dana.

Dana pushed me, and I stumbled into Ms. Cook, again. "Sorry again," I mumbled.

"You should find what you need in this section here," she said, smoothing out her dress. "Come back on Monday and I'll have more stuff for you."

"Umm, okay, that would be great, Ms. Cook," I said.

After she left, I started scanning the book spines. Dana grabbed one off the shelf and held it out to me.

"Look at this. It's a dictionary of Indian tribes."

I brought it to the checkout desk, and Ms. Cook turned it over twice, thumbing the pages.

"This one is really old. It should be in the reference section." She stamped the card inside and handed it back to me.

Dana and I sat on a bench in the schoolyard and looked through the book.

"It looks like it was printed a hundred years ago," she said.

"Look up *Mohawk*," I said.

Dana flipped the pages and we read together. The author said that the word *Mohawk* meant "man-eaters." There was a drawing of a brown man with an evil smile on his face and a thick strip of hair, holding up a scalp in one hand and a knife dripping with blood in the other.

Dana and I looked at each other, eyes wide. I slammed the book shut and shuddered.

THE next morning, Dana laughed as I pulled every piece of clothing from my chest of drawers and closet. "Just pick something already!"

"I have nothing to wear," I said.

"You have tons of clothes," Dana said as she sifted through the pile on my bed. "Here, wear these." She handed me a pair of dark jeans and a beige-and-navy-blue striped V-neck T-shirt. "They'll look great on you."

I tried the outfit on and modelled it in the mirror. "I don't know," I said, "these jeans are kinda tight."

"They're supposed to be tight. They look good on you."

"Dana's mother's here," Mom shouted from the kitchen.

"We'll be down in a minute," I shouted back.

"Eeee!" Dana shrieked. "Your first date with the man of your dreams. I'm so excited for you!"

I ran my hands over my hair to smooth it down. "How do I look?"

"Amazing."

We raced down the stairs, shouting goodbye to my mom, ran out the front door and climbed into Dana's mother's car.

DANA'S mother dropped us off at the entrance to the mall. "I'll pick you guys up at three thirty," she said.

"So," Dana said, once inside, "have fun! I'll meet you back here at three." She skipped away, turning once to wink and wave at me before disappearing.

I crossed the mall toward the coffee shop where I had arranged to meet Tommy. Just outside, I stopped and took a deep breath. I pushed through the glass doors and looked around. He wasn't in any of the booths. I decided to wait outside. Turning around, I almost knocked Tommy over. He had two coffee cups and held one out to me.

"Hi," he said.

IT was almost three thirty when I met Dana again.

"You're late," she scolded. "My mom's gonna be here any minute."

"I know, sorry."

"Yeah, well, you don't look sorry." She laughed. "I want all the juicy details."

"It was amazing. We spent the whole time talking."

"What did you talk about?"

"Nothing special. But Dana, I feel like I've known him my whole life. And he swears he knows me from somewhere. Everything felt so right being with him."

"Wow!" Dana said, dreamily.

"He's seventeen and already has his licence—which is a good thing, because he lives two hours away on an Indian reserve near Cornwall. Akwe . . . something. He told me ten times, but I can't remember how to pronounce it."

"He drove two hours to go on a date with you? Now I like him even more."

Just then, Tommy appeared out of nowhere.

"I forgot something," he said to me. Then he turned to Dana and smiled.

"Hey, Tommy," she said.

"Hi, Dana."

"I better go look for my mom. I'll see you out there, Carrie. Bye, Tommy." She left us alone.

"So what did you forget?" I asked.

"I forgot to say goodbye properly." He kissed me. A soft, gentle warm kiss. Then he touched my face and walked away.

MOM and Dad stepped into the hallway the second I closed the door.

"How was shopping with Dana?" Mom asked.

"Whoa! You scared me." I laughed. I was on cloud nine.

"How was shopping with Dana?" Mom asked again, an edge to her voice.

"Why so serious?"

"Answer your mother," Dad said sharply.

I'm busted. Do I confess or play dumb?

"Um . . ." I looked away for a moment, gathered my thoughts and decided to take my chances. "Shopping was good," I lied.

"You don't have any bags," Dad said, nodding toward my empty hands. "Didn't you find anything to buy?"

"Nnnooo," I said, drawing out the word. My stomach knotted up. I had a feeling I was about to get pelted.

Mom's expression changed from serious to deadly. Her eyebrow twitched. "One of my patients happened to mention that she saw you walking through a park in Perth today . . . with a tall boy."

I opened my mouth, but no words came out.

Mom's right foot tapped loudly.

"Oh crap," I muttered.

"What did you say?" Dad asked.

"Don't lie to us!" Mom exploded. "You were with that boy from the ice rink, weren't you?"

"We are so disappointed in you," Dad said.

Mom flailed her arms through the air and shouted something. But I wasn't listening to what she said. *They look like duelling orangutans from the National Geographic channel.*

That thought made me laugh.

Bad move.

"Go to your room!" Dad yelled.

I didn't wait to be told twice. I ducked around them and raced upstairs, closing the door behind me.

As I reached for the phone to call Dana, the door opened. Mom took the phone from my hands, pulling the cord from the wall. Dad unplugged my television and carried it out.

"You're grounded," Mom said.

"For how long?" I asked.

"Forever," she said, slamming the door.

BEING grounded on the weekend was no fun. No phone. No TV. All I could do was think about Tommy. *Okay, maybe being grounded isn't all that bad!*

The phone downstairs rang twice. Listening from my open bedroom door, I heard Mom tell Dana that I was grounded. When the phone rang again, she rudely told whoever called not to call back ever again. *Tommy.*

I was furious. *What right does she have?* To top it all off, they were trying to force me to go to another stupid science camp.

It's time to do something radical.

Chapter 5

*Rhythmic drumming. A dark-haired
woman lies motionless in a pool of blood.
An ambulance worker pulls a sheet up
over her. Behind them is the wrecked
heap of a car. A fireman reaches into
the back seat and pulls out something
wrapped in a crumpled blanket, handing
it off behind him. Then he reaches in
again and pulls out another tiny bundle.
The rhythmic drumming grows louder,
masking the faint sound of babies crying.*

I WOKE UP MONDAY MORNING WITH MY HEART POUNDING.
Another car-crash dream. *Will someone else die?*

Mom had already gone to work. She left me a frozen waffle
and a note.

*I love you very much, Carrie, but you're still grounded.
Come straight home after school. Since you leave for*

science camp on Sunday, you can see Dana this week, but only at home. Good luck with your math exam.

I left the waffle uneaten and called Dana. "Can you come over before school?"

"Be right there."

I went up to my bedroom to get changed. I dug through my top drawer and pulled out my bank book. I had six hundred and forty-three dollars and twenty-seven cents to my name.

That's enough to last me a long time.

Dana barged into my bedroom. She had one pant leg tucked into her sock, and her T-shirt was all wrinkled. Her blonde hair was pulled up in a bun on top of her head. Loose strands of hair danced wildly around her face.

"I'm dying to find out what happened with Tommy after I left," Dana said, breathless, "and why you've been put under lock and key for life."

"Someone saw . . ."

"Wait!" Dana interrupted. "Tommy first."

"He kissed me."

"Wow! How was it?"

I smiled and nodded.

"That's so exciting. When are you going to see him again?"

"According to my mom and dad, never. One of Mom's patients saw me with him and told her. They went ballistic and grounded me forever. But I've got a plan. There's more than one reason that I need to see Tommy. I've been dreaming about the woman with the long dark hair again. I think she's going to get hurt. I've got to find her. Maybe Tommy can help."

"Oh my God, that's horrible! So what's your plan?"

"Do you promise not to tell?"

"This doesn't sound good."

"Promise?"

"Okay, fine," she said.

"Say the words."

"I promise not to tell."

"I'm going to run away. I'm leaving after math exam this morning. It's our last exam. Then I'm finished with school."

"What? Where? That's crazy."

"I'll take the Greyhound to Cornwall and call Tommy. He'll help me for sure."

"For real?"

"Yeah. For real. I have over six hundred dollars saved up."

"Don't you think that's a bit drastic?"

"Besides, I'm being shipped off to science camp again."

"Oh yeah . . . science camp."

"I need to find some answers, and Mom and Dad will never help me."

"I'll go with you."

"No, this is my problem, not yours."

"There's no way I'm letting you run off by yourself. Either I'm coming with you or you're staying here."

"Okay, fine. You can come. Thanks, Dana," I said, hugging her. "You're the best."

AFTER we finished our math exam, Dana and I went to the bank where I withdrew all my savings.

"This is exciting," Dana said, "in a scary kind of way."

"When we get to Cornwall, Tommy will pick us up."

AT the bus depot, the ticketing agent was sitting behind the counter reading a newspaper.

"Two tickets to Cornwall, please," I said.

"The bus leaves in one hour," the attendant said without looking up. "Boarding starts in forty-five minutes."

When she lifted her eyes, she froze for a moment and stared. Then she looked over at Dana. "Do you two have permission to be travelling on your own?"

"Of course," I said. "We're going to visit our aunt. She's meeting us at the bus station."

Eventually she pushed two tickets across the counter.

"Let's sit here," I said to Dana, dropping my backpack down in front of a couple of dirty chairs.

Dana plopped hers beside mine and sat down. "Only forty minutes to wait."

"I'm really nervous."

I looked around the bus station. A woman sat with her teenage daughter. The daughter had her eyes closed and played air drums. The mother whispered something to her, and the girl put her hands on her lap and sat still.

Lots of people moved back and forth through the bus station. Finally our boarding announcement came over the loudspeaker. "Bus to Cornwall now boarding on Platform 7."

Dana poked me in the arm as I bent to grab my backpack. "Carrie, don't look back."

"Why?" I said, turning around.

"I said don't look!" she whispered.

There was a cop holding a flyer in his hand. He was standing by the ticket counter talking to the attendant, who was pointing right at me.

"Oh crap. Crap, crap, crap," Dana groaned.

"Don't look nervous, Dana. Just keep your cool."

The officer walked toward us. I tried to stay calm, but my stomach knotted up. "Hi, girls," he said. "Where are we off to?"

His voice was friendly, but his eyes were like searchlights.

"Umm . . ." I could feel my face getting red. "Cornwall."

"Hmmm," he said. "Do your parents know?"

"Sure," I said, trying to keep calm. "We're going to visit our aunt."

Just then Dana started making weird noises in her throat. I shot her a warning glance, but it was too late. "We're not running away! Oh please don't tell our parents!"

The police officer held up the flyer, his eyes darting back and forth.

"Jessica, you and your friend need to come with me."

"I'm not Jessica."

He showed me the flyer—a missing person poster.

"Tell me this isn't you, young lady. It sure looks like you."

I looked at the photo of the girl on the flyer.

It *was* me.

Chapter 6

THE OFFICER USHERED DANA AND ME INTO THE FRONT lobby of the police station. He gestured to a row of metal chairs against the wall, and we sat down sheepishly.

"That girl in the poster looks just like me."

"I know . . . freaky," Dana said. Tears welled up in her eyes. "They're gonna call our parents, aren't they?"

"Probably."

She sighed. "Looks like I'll be getting grounded forever too."

"Dana, don't you think it's weird that there's someone out there who looks exactly like me?"

"Yeah, sure is."

The policeman at the front desk was talking on the phone. I could only catch a few words. "Runaway . . . missing person . . . the girl's father . . . it has to be her . . . look at the photo . . ."

"This is ridiculous," I fumed. "I'm not missing. I'm right here."

I thought about my dreams—the ones where I am drumming along with a strange man, the ones where I have a mole on my arm. *Maybe the girl in the dreams isn't me.*

"Dana, the girl in the poster must be my twin sister."

Oh my God, she's missing! And I need to find her.

I jumped out of my chair and raced to the desk. "Excuse me," I said to the policeman. He held up his hand like a stop sign and continued talking on the phone.

Just then a woman pushed through the front door. Her long brown hair was a mess, and her shirt was only half tucked in. She wore a black knit sweater over her dress shirt and blue jeans. She was carrying two McDonald's bags.

"Hi, Carrie. Hi, Dana," she said, walking over to us and extending her hand. "I'm Bethany Davies, a social worker. Please call me Beth."

We each shook her hand.

"Sorry, I'm a mess," she laughed. "Today was supposed to be my day off. Big Macs okay?"

She handed us the brown bags. We nodded.

"Come with me, Carrie," she said. "Dana, you wait here. Your parents are on the way."

"Shit," said Dana under her breath, loud enough for me to hear.

Beth led me into a back room and nodded to a chair. I sat down, dug into the McDonald's bag, grabbed a burger and took a big bite.

"So, here we are. Do you have any idea why the police brought you in?"

"Because I was sneaking away to meet my boyfriend?" I mumbled through a mouthful of food.

She held up the missing person flyer. "No. It's because you look just like this girl."

"It's not me," I said. "Did she run away too?"

"Yes, she did, but she's gone back home."

"Then why am I here now?"

"We're waiting for your parents to pick you up."

"Science camp is looking pretty good right about now," I mumbled, sitting back and folding my arms across my chest.

A policewoman opened the door and peeked in. "Ms. Davies, the Stowes are here."

My parents walked in. The room began to feel very small.

My mom hissed. "We have a lot to talk about, missy." She raised an eyebrow and sat down beside me.

The social worker stood up. "Mrs. and Mr. Stowe, I'm Beth Davies. Mr. Stowe, please take a seat. We have some information about Carrie that will come as a shock."

"I think I have a twin sister," I blurted. I turned to Beth. "Where is she? Where is my sister?"

"She's back home with her father," Beth said. "His name is Harold Williams. It seems he's your biological father too. He's been looking for you for years."

Tears streamed down my cheeks. My mother touched my arm, but I shrugged her off. "Tell me about him."

"He's Mohawk. He lives on an Indian reservation near Montreal. Your sister's name is Jessica. She's the girl on the poster."

Beth passed the poster to me.

I studied my sister's face.

"When the police found you, they called Harold. But he said Jessica had returned home safe and sound. He knew all about you, but he hadn't been able to find you, up to now. So it was good luck you ran away."

"Good luck?" Mom said.

Beth ignored the question and carried on. "When he found out that he had fathered twin girls, he began looking for you and Jessica. Jessica was eleven at the time and still in foster care. There was no information about you."

"We had no idea anyone was looking for her," Dad said.

The theme songs for *The Twilight Zone* and *The Young and the Restless* suddenly popped into my mind.

My biological father!

"Mr. Williams wants to meet you, Carrie. Do you want to meet him too?"

"Yes. I do."

Chapter 7

*A fireball arcs through the air and lands
with a loud bang. The force of the explosion
shakes the ground violently. I hunch down
behind a small shrub, my hand over my
mouth, my body rocking from side to side.
Slow, rhythmic drumming grows louder
and louder. Through watery, burning eyes
I see people running. Explosions erupt all
around us. A man topples over and lies still.
A scream pierces the air. My eyes sting and
I close them tight. Someone is rocking me
back and forth, back and forth.*

I OPENED MY EYES. IT WAS MY MOM, SHAKING ME AWAKE.

"Carrie, you were screaming in your sleep," Mom said,
looking worried.

"It was just a dream," I mumbled.

"C'mon, get dressed. You have to go over to the school and
clean out your locker. Then we have to go meet Ms. Davies at

the Children's Aid Society. Dad and I will meet you in front of the school at eleven thirty."

"CAN you believe it?" I said to Dana, as we cleaned out our lockers. "I am Mohawk, same as Tommy."

"And you have a twin sister too. Meanwhile I've been grounded for the whole summer."

Just then Ms. Cook came up. "Carrie, here," she said, handing me a photocopy. "I found an article that you might find interesting."

"Thanks, Ms. Cook," I said, taking it.

I sat down on a bench to read it. There was a picture of a Mohawk woman with a caption:

"THESE GROUNDS HAVE BEEN SACRED TO US FOR CENTURIES. WE ARE PREPARED TO FIGHT, AND EVEN DIE, TO PROTECT OUR LAND. THE GOLF COURSE DOESN'T BELONG HERE."

I'm Mohawk. Maybe I'm supposed to fight too.

"I've got to go," Dana said, nudging me. "I've got to go meet Josh."

"Sure," I said, looking at the clock in the hall. "Mom and Dad will be outside by now."

"HURRY up, get in," Mom said through the open car window.

I got into the back seat, and Dad started up the car. We drove in silence, until we reached a grim, red brick building in the middle of nowhere.

Beth was waiting for us in the lobby. She looked impeccable. Her hair was tied back in a slick ponytail, and she wore a grey pantsuit with white pinstripes. Black pointy high heels poked out beneath the hem of her trouser legs. "Harold's here," she said, ushering us along. "He's waiting for us in the family room."

Mom, me and Dad followed behind her like a trail of ducklings.

When we entered the room, a tall man rose and smiled.

Beth gestured to us. "Harold, this is your daughter, Carrie, and her adoptive parents, Katherine and Johnathan Stowe." She turned to me. "Carrie, this is your biological father, Harold Williams."

Beth sat down at a table, and Harold stepped forward, holding out both his hands. I took them and squeezed tightly.

He has a dimple in his chin just like me.

"I've been dreaming about this moment for years," Harold said, pulling out a picture from his shirt pocket. He passed it to me. "This is Jessica. Five years ago I didn't know I had even one daughter. Now the Creator has blessed me with two beautiful girls."

We all sat down.

"Have you found my mother too?" I said. Mom shot me a look. "I mean . . . my biological mother?"

"Well," Beth said, her jaw muscles twitching as she flipped through an open file. "Her name was Deborah Swanson."

"Was?" I asked. My heart sank.

"I'm so sorry, Carrie. She was killed in a car accident shortly after you and your sister were born." *Just like in my dreams.* "You and Jessica were in the car with her. Luckily a fireman pulled you and your sister to safety. The authorities couldn't find any family, so both of you were put up for adoption."

My stomach knotted. *Now I'll never meet her.* I felt like throwing up.

Harold broke in. "I'm sorry I didn't find you then, Carrie. I didn't know anything about you and your sister. Deborah was from a different reserve. We were dating for two years, and I was madly in love with her. But one day out of the blue, she told me it was over. I was devastated, so I moved to New York to work with my cousin as an ironworker on the skyscrapers."

There was an awkward silence. Finally Beth began to finish the story. "Deborah moved to Toronto, and you and your sister were born there. That's where the accident happened. You were adopted, but Jessica ended up in foster care until Harold found her."

"Jessica and I," Harold said, "moved in with my mother in Kahnawake."

Holy cow, I have a grandmother too.

"I can't wait to introduce you to your sister." Harold beamed.

"Mom, why didn't you and Dad adopt us both?"

"Honey, we didn't know about your sister until today."

"We love you more than anything in the world," Dad added.

"Unfortunately," Beth said, "sometimes siblings were separated back then. I am truly sorry."

"Why wasn't Jessica adopted by someone else?"

Beth flipped through her file again. "She was injured in the car accident and had to undergo a series of surgeries. The doctors were also monitoring some developmental delays that may have resulted from the accident. People are sometimes scared off by, how do I say it . . . complications. By the time Jessica was given a clean bill of health, she was almost four. It appears she got lost in the system."

"We love you more than anything," Mom blurted out, dabbing at her eyes with a balled up tissue.

Dad leaned back in his chair, his eyes closed and his hands clenched tightly together.

"Will you come home with me to meet the rest of your family?" Harold asked. He turned, first to Mom and then to Dad. "Would that be okay with you, Mr. and Mrs. Stowe?"

"Call me Katherine," Mom said.

"And please, call me Johnathan," Dad added.

"This must be difficult for you," Beth said, turning to Mom and Dad.

"Mom. Dad. Please let me go. I want to meet my birth family."

"Well . . ." Dad said, "you have science camp."

"And it's so far away," Mom said.

I started to cry.

"Maybe for a weekend . . ."

"At least a week," I demanded through my tears.

"But science camp starts on Monday," Dad persisted.

"Dad, this is so much more important than science camp."

"I know," he said. His face turned a ghostly white. A drop of sweat dripped from his brow and down his cheek.

Mom touched Dad's hand, and her expression softened. "Okay, Carrie, you can go . . . but only for a week."

Harold opened his arms and swept me up in a bear hug.

Chapter 8

I am running, following Jessica. Branches scratch me, and I try to protect my face as we run blindly through the dark woods. "We have to hurry!" I yell. A drum beats rhythmically, each beat matching my steps. Startled by an explosion, I suddenly trip and feel blood trickle down my leg. "Hurry, we might already be too late!" I shout to Jessica.

IT WAS SATURDAY MORNING, A WEEK LATER. DANA WAS sitting on my bed, watching me pack. "Jeez Louise, so much stuff, you're only going for a week."

"Maybe I'll stay the summer."

"What about science camp?"

"I'm never going to another science camp ever."

"Carrie!" Mom called from downstairs. "We're waiting for you." Her voice was shrill.

Dana gave me a hug. "Call me as soon as you can, okay?"

"Okay, sure. I'll miss you."

WE drove in silence. I thought about the picture in the dictionary. Man-eaters. I shuddered. Eventually I dozed off.

*I stand in-between two groups of people
shouting at each other. A rock, a beer bottle, all
kinds of garbage fly through the air. The man
with the bandana is dressed in camouflage.
He is standing atop a pile of tires and waving
a gun in the air. A drum beats. A white bird
swoops down. A shot rings out and the man
tumbles down. Screams. More gun shots.
Bodies drop. The man with the bandana is
dead. I reach down to uncover his face.*

WE hit a bump in the road.

"Where are we?" I asked Dad.

"We're on the Mercier Bridge. We're almost there."

I looked down at the water far below. The river churned violently, breaking in white crests along the shore. Something about the bridge filled me with dread.

A short while later, we pulled into a long driveway and up to a small brown house. It had a wraparound porch. We parked next to a row of cars.

I took a deep breath, stepped out and walked toward the

front door. Mom and Dad followed. The door opened. Harold was standing in the doorway next to an elderly woman. He wore a white T-shirt with a small feather design above his heart. He stepped forward and hugged me. He turned around. "Carrie, this is your grandmother."

She has the same dimple as me. Her eyes sparkled, and a smile filled her wrinkled face. She had short, wavy black hair.

"Carrie! We've been waiting for you all these years." She pulled me close and smothered my face in the crook of her neck. "Call me Gramma."

"Ma, these are Carrie's parents, Johnathan and Katherine," Harold said, gesturing. Mom waved half-heartedly, and Dad gave her a weak smile.

"And you call me Ma," Gramma said. She grabbed their hands and pulled them inside. "Come in, come in."

She hollered over her shoulder, "They're here!"

There was a wild commotion—chair legs scraping against the floor, footsteps thundering along the hall, talking, laughing, voices blending together. A troop of people charged into the front hall and bombarded me with hugs. Mom and Dad flattened themselves against the wall.

"Okay, that's enough. Everyone back off." Gramma swatted her arms around. "Give the girl some room to breathe. Everyone go in the kitchen and get ready for dinner."

"I'm so happy to have you as family," Harold said to Mom and Dad after everyone had cleared the hallway.

Dad swallowed audibly, and Mom murmured something unintelligible under her breath.

Harold turned to me. "Carrie, come with me. You have your own room. I'll show it to you."

He led me down the hall into a tiny bedroom. It had a small chest of drawers, and light flooded in through the window. It was cheerful.

"I moved a few walls around to make your room," he said, pointing to the walls.

"You moved the walls?"

"Yes, your grandmother likes renovating, so I built this house with moveable walls to make it easier whenever she decides to shake things up. Pretty handy."

"Wow, a room built just for me."

"I want you to know you can stay here with us for as long as you want, whenever you like. You're not a visitor, you're family."

Family.

"Thank you." I hugged him, and we joined the others in the kitchen. Delicious smells greeted me, and my stomach rumbled.

Everyone—my aunts, uncles, cousins and who knows who else—bustled around an extra-long table. I counted at least seventeen people.

Then I saw her in the doorway. Jessica. She looked exactly like me, except for the mole on her right arm.

Harold called her over. "Jessica, come and meet your sister, Carrie, and her parents."

Jessica sat down at the far end of the table, looked up and waved weakly.

"Here, Carrie," Gramma said, scooping something out of a steaming pot and dumping it into a bowl. "Chicken and dumplings."

Then she scraped up a giant patty and a gravy-covered

steak, sliding them onto a plate. "Cornbread and steak . . . and meat pie!" she said, piling on a thick slice and smothering everything with ketchup.

I sat down between Harold and Dad, placing the bowl and the plate down on the table in front of me. Mom was seated on the other side of Dad.

Harold went around the table and introduced me to all my relatives. I tried to remember their names but it was hopeless.

"The Creator brought her home," Aunt Becky announced. Everyone nodded.

"I'm the luckiest man in the world," Harold said, nodding first at me and then at Jessica, before helping himself to another slice of meat pie. "Great dinner, Ma."

Gramma placed a steaming mug of tea in front of me. Slivers of tree bark floated in it. "Drink up," Gramma said. "Ginseng tea. It's good for you." She smiled and sipped from her own mug.

Everyone was talking at once, and every few seconds someone would break out into a huge belly laugh. It was overwhelming.

"Remember that buffet we found when we were working in New York?" someone at the end of the table shouted.

"Oh yeah, and the sign said ALL YOU CAN EAT $6.99. We thought we hit the jackpot," a guy sitting across from me shouted back.

"We went there four nights in a row and cleaned out the buffet each time. We go back a fifth night and the sign's changed. Now it says, ALL YOU CAN EAT $6.99 (UNLESS YOU'RE FROM KAHNAWAKE, THEN IT'S $29.99)."

Everyone roared. The table shook.

"Eat up," Gramma said, leaning over to me. "You're so skinny."

I picked up a dumpling and popped it into my mouth. It felt like a slimy oyster slipping down my throat.

"Delicious, isn't it?" Gramma smiled. "It's an old family recipe."

"Mhmn . . ." I nodded and smiled back.

"Carrie's such a wonderful girl," Gramma said to my parents. "You've done a great job raising her."

Mom didn't answer. "I think we have to leave now." She stood up abruptly. "It's a long drive home." She turned to Gramma. "Thank you so much for such a lovely dinner."

I followed them to the front door.

"Are you sure you want to stay, Carrie?" Mom asked.

"Yeah, I'm sure."

"We'll pick you up next week," Dad said.

They hugged me and left.

Chapter 9

I am in a taxi, going home to McDonalds Corners. As we drive away, Gramma's house grows smaller and smaller in the rear-view mirror. A white bird flies past the car toward the house. A gunshot rings out, and the white bird falls to the ground. It's dead. A siren shrieks. I shout to the driver to stop, but he doesn't listen—he taps on the steering wheel with a drumstick, and the drumming sound grows louder and louder.

I WOKE IN A COLD SWEAT. FOR A MOMENT I DIDN'T KNOW where I was. I grabbed my notepad and jotted down the crazy dream I just had.

I went into the kitchen. Gramma and Harold were speaking in low voices at the table. They stopped talking when I came into the room.

"Good morning, Carrie," Gramma said.

"Good morning." I smiled. "Hmmm, can I make a phone call?"

"Of course you can, this is your home now," Harold said. "Want to call your parents?"

The thought hadn't even occurred to me. "N-no," I stammered, feeling embarrassed. "Actually, it's a . . . a friend I need to call."

Gramma gave me a funny look. "You go right ahead. C'mon, Harold, help me water the garden."

After they left I picked up the phone and dialled Tommy.

IT took forever for Tommy to get there. I waited impatiently on the couch, staring out the window for what seemed like hours. Finally a clunky old Chevette pulled into the driveway.

The doorbell rang and Harold opened the door. "Hi, Tommy," he said. "What brings you here?"

"He's going to show me around the reserve," I piped in.

Tommy was wearing the same ball cap that he wore when I met him at the mall, the one with the little white bird.

The white bird in my dreams.

"Coach Williams," Tommy said, "great to see you again." He held out his hand. "Carrie and I met at a hockey tournament a while ago."

Harold turned to Carrie. "I coached Tommy's hockey team a few years ago. Jessica used to come along to watch us practise. Tommy, how's your brother?"

"He's still scoring lots of goals," Tommy said. "Is it okay with you if I take Carrie for the day?"

"Sure," said Harold. "Have a good time, but be careful. There's trouble brewing."

"I know all about it. Don't worry, I'll be careful. Ready, Carrie?"

I nodded. "Bye, Gramma," I shouted down the hall.

Mom and Dad would not be pleased.

TOMMY and I chatted and listened to music as he drove.

I pointed to a video recorder in the back of the car. "That looks pretty professional."

"I want to be ready in case a good story pops up."

"Are you some kind of reporter?"

"Sort of. A few of my stories have been broadcast on our local channel, nothing big."

"What kind of stories?"

"Nothin' major. But one day I'm gonna get a really big story. That's why I keep the camera with me all the time. So I'll be ready."

"Wow, that's so cool."

"Yeah, in September I'm going to journalism school."

"Where?"

"Maybe Toronto. I'm on a waiting list."

"What's it like living on a reserve?"

"Same as anywhere. Kahnawake's pretty big compared to most reserves. Down over there is the main part of town. It runs along the St. Lawrence Seaway. That's where most of the houses and businesses are. The road we're on leads to the Mercier Bridge. But I'll take the exit just before the bridge and show you the town. The area where your Gramma lives, just beside Chateguay, they call 'the farm'."

"The farm?"

"Yeah, there are only a few houses on that part of the reserve."

We turned off the exit and I saw an advertisement for a golf course. I thought about the article from Miss Cook. "Are there any golf courses here?"

"Yeah, a couple," Tommy answered. "You play golf?"

"No," I shook my head. "Do you?"

"A little."

"What did Harold mean about trouble brewing?"

"It's because of the golf course."

"Is that the cemetery thing?"

"So you've heard about it?"

"Yeah, I read an article about it."

Tommy's thumb tapped the steering wheel in rhythm to the music on the radio. "There are protests starting, but not right here. At least, not yet. The main protest is in Kanehsatake. I might get a good story there." He turned toward me and smiled.

I shivered.

No one was there when I got back, and when I tried calling Dana, there was no answer. So I went to my room to read. But I fell fast asleep instead.

I walk into the bathroom and flip on the light switch. Stepping in front of the sink, I look in the mirror. Startled, I step back. I'm wearing a dark turtleneck and a dark cap. A bandana covers my face. Only my eyes are visible. Blood trickles from the corners of my eyes. I raise my hand to wipe it away and see in the mirror that I'm holding a gun.

"**WANT** to learn how to make cornbread?" Gramma asked, waking me up.

"Sure," I said, rubbing the sleep from my eyes.

I picked my book up off the floor and followed her to the kitchen.

"First we pour some cornmeal into a bowl." She tipped some flour from a bag into a measuring cup.

"Gramma, that's flour, not cornmeal."

Gramma put the bag close to her eyes and squinted. Her nose was just inches from the label. "So it is." She laughed as she dug into the cupboard, pulled out another bag and shook it. "Shoot. It's almost empty."

"Is there a store nearby? I'll go get some," I offered.

"Such a good girl," Gramma said, smiling. She pulled some money out of her purse. "It's a short walk straight down the main road into Chateguay. You'll see the grocery store on the right, just past the intersection."

"No problem, Gramma."

I stood in the aisle trying to choose which cornmeal Gramma might like. I felt someone's hands slide over my eyes. "Hello, gorgeous," a boy whispered into my ear, his lips grazing my neck. "I love it when you wear your hair up."

I jerked away and turned around.

"Hey, hey, it's just me, Jess." His black hair was buzzed really short. He stood about half a foot taller than me. His biceps bulged right out of his T-shirt.

"I'm not Jess," I said, freaked out.

"Oh, no way." He laughed. "You must be Jess' sister, Carrie. Sorry about that. I'm Nate, her boyfriend."

He held out his hand and I shook it.

"Nice to meet you," I said.

"You're definitely identical, like everyone says."

"Jessica doesn't give me the time of day."

He lowered his voice and looked at me out of one eye. "Don't worry, she'll come around."

"Hey, Nate, let's go!" someone shouted from down the aisle. Two boys stood there waving.

"Gotta run. See you around."

At the cash register, I spotted Jessica staring at me through the store window, her eyes narrowed.

I waved. But by the time I got outside, she was gone.

I handed Gramma the bag of cornmeal. She squinted at the bag, lifting it close to her face. "Perfect," she said, smiling.

Then she showed me how to make cornbread and dumplings. As we worked, she taught me some words in

Mohawk. They were hard to pronounce, but Gramma repeated them patiently until I got them right.

As we shaped the dumplings, Gramma talked about her life. She told me about her children, grandchildren and great-grandchildren. She talked about the Creator, and about the St. Lawrence River before the seaway was built. "I remember as a young girl, before the seaway came along, our river was pure and clean to swim in. We also drank the water from the river. It was a playground for all our family, relatives and friends."

Sometimes she'd switch from English to Mohawk. Her voice was so soothing and peaceful. It didn't matter if I didn't understand everything she said.

Soon the kitchen filled with delicious smells.

"Your grandfather was a sky-walker."

"What's a sky-walker?"

"Ahh," she said, a smile creeping across her face. "That's what we call ironworkers. Our men are very brave. They walk across thin steel beams fifty stories high to build skyscrapers and bridges. Your grandfather built a lot of buildings in New York. Sometimes he would come home only once or twice a month."

"You must have missed him."

"We all help each other here. Your father is a sky-walker too. He worked on the World Trade Center."

A sky-walker. I thought about my dream where a shadow man dances in the sun across a tightrope. The hairs on my arms prickled.

"Where does the name *Mohawk* come from? I read in a book that it means 'man-eaters.'"

"It is a name given to us by other nations long ago when our lives were filled with war—before the Great Peace. Be careful what you read. You can let other people define you or you can choose to define yourself. Some of our people are offended by the name *Mohawk*, and others are offended by the name *Indian*. To me, a name doesn't matter. I'm Kanien'keha:ka, I'm Mohawk, I'm Indian, I'm Native. What matters is that our people remain strong. We have a powerful history, a rich culture and proud traditions."

"That gives me a lot to think about."

Gramma bent over and wrapped her arms around me. "You don't have to figure it all out right now. I want to know about you too. Do you know how to sew?"

"A little," I answered.

"A little's no good. I'll teach you how to sew."

AFTER the cornbread was baked, we settled down on the couch. Gramma opened an old cookie tin filled with pins and needles and thread and beads. She showed me how to cut pieces of leather, sew them together and bead them. In no time she held up the most beautiful little booties with beaded flower designs on top.

"Moccasins," she said proudly. "Now you try."

"Oh no, I can't do that. They're beautiful."

"You can do it," Gramma said, encouraging me.

IT took me forever but I managed to sew some little boots together. I held them up just as Jessica walked in.

"Not very good," Jessica said, shaking her head.

One moccasin was bigger than the other, and threads were hanging down everywhere.

"You're right, Jess. They are pretty sad looking."

"My name is Jessica," she said coldly.

"Oh, sorry."

"Would you like to sew with us, Jessica?" Gramma asked.

"No thanks, Gramma. I have to call Nate." She shot me a nasty look. "Apparently some girl was hitting on him at the grocery today."

Then she disappeared down the hall.

"Don't worry," Gramma said, "she'll warm up. She needs time."

She added our moccasins to a pile of stuff in the corner of the living room.

"What's all that for?"

"They're gifts for my new great-grandbaby." She pulled out a bunting bag with fake fur trim, embroidered with wolf and bear shapes. "Jessica made this one."

"Wow, it's beautiful." I sighed.

"Jessica's really talented," Gramma said. "She does beautiful beadwork. Go find her and tell her dinner's almost ready. She's probably in her room."

Gramma was right. Jessica was in her room reading.

"Mind if I come in?" I asked from the doorway.

"Whatever," she said, without looking up from her book.

I stepped in. "Gramma showed me the bunting bag and moccasins you made. They're really beautiful."

"Thanks," she said, nonplussed. "Gramma taught me how to sew when I first moved here. My first few pairs of moccasins were awful." She paused. "Although, nowhere near as bad as yours."

"They are pretty bad." I laughed. "Your boyfriend is really nice."

"You think so?" she said, giving me an icy look.

"Well . . . Gramma said to come for dinner." I turned and walked out of the bedroom without waiting for an answer.

I went back to the kitchen. No one was there, so I decided to call my parents. I didn't really want to, but I thought I should. No one answered.

I think I'll call Dana.

"Carrie!" Dana shrieked, picking up at her end. "What's going on? Tell me everything!"

"It's hard to explain."

"What's your sister like?"

"I haven't talked to her much. I've tried, but she's really distant. Gramma's great. Harold is too. He built me my own room, and Gramma's teaching me how to cook and sew. I'm even learning how to speak Mohawk."

"Sounds like you're having fun."

"I'm still having those dreams. I've been dreaming like crazy since I got here."

"Is it the same guy with the gun?"

"Yeah, and the same white bird too. Someone is going to get hurt, I know it."

"I hope not."

"I hope not too. But I'm not going back home until I figure all of this stuff out."

Chapter 10

I'm crawling along the ground toward a man with a bandana covering his face. He is lying motionless beside a pile of tires. I reach for him and pull off the bandana. There is a mirror where his face should have been. I see my own reflection there.

I AWOKE THE NEXT MORNING TO THE SMELL OF SMOKE.
Fire!

I sat up in bed and saw Gramma kneeling on the floor next to me, chanting. She was waving a feather across an earthen bowl, sending curls of smoke dancing through the air.

"Gramma, what are you doing?"

"Hush. The medicines are healing."

"Medicines?"

"Yes, sage, sweetgrass and tobacco."

"You use cigarettes to pray?"

"Dried tobacco leaves," she whispered. "The tobacco smoke carries my prayers of thanks to the Creator in the spirit world; the sage removes bad energy; and the sweetgrass, sacred hair of Mother Earth, brings good energy."

Smoke danced up to the ceiling.

Gramma was so small, especially kneeling down, yet her presence filled the entire room. I felt love in my heart. I felt safe. I started to cry. Tears streamed down my cheeks.

I had a shower and sat down for breakfast.

Gramma placed a steaming mug of tea in front of me and sat down. "Our medicines are very powerful, Carrie. Some carry our prayers to the Creator, some heal our bodies and some keep us from getting sick. Each one of us is made up of mind, body, spirit and emotion. We are connected to the earth in the same way as we are connected to our families. Our sacred medicines will nourish you and protect you. I reconnect with nature every day when I walk through the forest. It recharges me emotionally and spiritually. It fuels my soul."

Just like when I walk through the forest by myself.

I sipped my tea. *I wonder what Mom and Dad would think of Gramma's medicines.*

Harold walked in, smiling. "Good morning." He kissed the top of my head and squeezed my shoulder, like it was a normal everyday thing.

"Ma, you ready to go?" He piled eggs and bacon on his plate. "Jessica!" he shouted. "Get out here, hun. Breakfast is getting cold."

"Your dad's driving me to the mall," Gramma said. "Do you want to come shopping?"

"Yeah, that sounds great."

"Are you sure you're up for it? Gramma's shopping trips are legendary."

"I'm up for anything," I said, looking hopefully down the hallway.

Jessica didn't appear.

JUST after we left the reserve, a cop flashed his lights and we pulled over to the side of the road.

Harold rolled down his window.

The cop leaned in, speaking rapid-fire French.
"What's the problem, officer?" Harold asked.

He answered angrily in heavily accented English. "Licence, registration and insurance."

Harold handed the policeman the registration, taking his licence out of his wallet. The cop grabbed them and spat out, "You were speeding."

Harold said nothing. I could see a vein pulsing on his temple.

"You were going over seventy in a sixty zone."

That doesn't seem right. We weren't going that fast.

"I'll be back," the cop said, retreating to his car.

"We weren't going that fast, Harold," I said.

He turned around. "I know. There are a few cops around here who have a problem with us because we're Mohawk. They find any reason to pull us over, and even make stuff up."

"That's terrible. You shouldn't let him do that to you."

"There's no point fighting them," Gramma said. "It's better to let it go and work as a community. That way we can spread understanding and get along with each other."

The cop returned and thrust a ticket through the open window, muttering something in French.

AT the entrance to Walmart, Harold said, "I'll pick you up at five."

"Five?"

"Yep. I warned you." He winked at me and pulled away.

Gramma grabbed a cart. "You get one too."

"Oh, I don't need anything."

"Not for you, for me," she said, passing me her cart and grabbing another for herself.

We walked around the store, aisle by aisle, until the carts were full—children's pyjamas, bath towels, colouring books, work boots, T-shirts, soap, board games, socks of all colours, rolls of paper towels and three basketballs.

Gramma paid, and we jammed our bagged goods into one cart. As I pushed it out of the store, I bumped into an older man dressed in a Hawaiian shirt.

"Oops, sorry," I said, jumping to catch one of the bags that was tumbling over.

"Damned Indians," he said, glaring at me.

I felt my face flush and wished the ground would swallow me up. Gramma glared back at him until he looked away. "Keep your head up, Carrie. Be proud of who you are."

Who am I? I don't even know. This would never happen to me back home.

I kept my head up like she told me.

We ate lunch at the food court—cannelloni—then spent the rest of the afternoon choosing backsplash tiles for

Gramma's kitchen. I filled the cart with twenty packages of tiles, three different times. Each time, after the cart was loaded, she changed her mind. Finally, happy with her fourth choice, she went to the checkout and paid.

Harold was waiting for us when we stepped into the parking lot with our loaded carts. "You survived," he said, laughing, as he piled everything into the trunk.

Chapter 11

I hear shouting and drumming. I get out of bed and weave my way in the dark through the living room and out the front door. The drumming is drowned out by the sound of crunching metal. Men in camouflage are crouched behind piles of tires and crushed cars scattered around the road. A man with a bandana covering everything but his eyes stands atop a pile of tires and raises a rifle. A burst of fire arcs toward him. "No!" I scream, scaling the pile of tires. I push the man out of the way, just as the fireball hits me. A white bird flies up and soars high into the sky.

I WOKE UP TO GRAMMA'S VOICE DRIFTING IN FROM THE kitchen. As I went for breakfast, I stumbled over an empty box. Several more were strewn across the floor.

"What's going on?" I asked Gramma.

"I put the tiles up. But they look crooked, don't you think?"

Yep, definitely crooked. "No, looks fine to me. I can't believe you did all that this morning."

"I wanted to get the tiling done right away. It was fun shopping with you yesterday. I'm so happy you're here with us."

"What happened to your hand?" I asked, noticing a bandage.

"I cut it peeling apples earlier this morning. It's nothing."

Someone coughed behind me. It was Jessica, standing in the doorway with her arms crossed.

Harold came up behind her holding two bags bursting with ears of corn. He emptied them onto the kitchen table. "Here you go, girls. Direct from the garden."

He put his arm around Jessica and drew her into the kitchen. Then he took me under his other arm. "This is a dream come true. My two beautiful girls together."

Jessica grabbed an ear of corn and began tearing at the husk.

I reached for a garbage bag in the cupboard.

"No, no," Gramma said. "We're going to use the husks."

"For what?"

"To make dolls. And tea. Jessica, show Carrie how to make a corn-husk doll. I'll start on the tea." Gramma pulled the stringy corn hairs and dropped them into a pot of boiling water, while Jessica started making a doll with the husks.

Within minutes Jessica was finished.

"It's beautiful. It's better than any doll in a toy store."

"Now you try, Carrie," Gramma said, smiling. She handed me a bunch of corn husks.

I tried to copy what Jessica had done, but my doll fell apart. I watched Jessica make one perfect doll after another.

Gramma poured the corn-hair tea into mugs and put them on the table in front of us.

I took a sip. *Hmm, not bad.*

I tried again and again to make a doll. Finally, I made one that didn't fall apart.

"Jessica, show Carrie all the other dolls you've made."

Jessica smiled. "Sure. Follow me."

Corn-husk dolls were everywhere in her room. Some had realistic hair and outfits with detailed beadwork and tiny moccasins.

"Wow," I said. "You made all these?"

"Yeah."

"They're beautiful."

"Thanks."

"You could sell these. They're really good." I took a deep breath. "I've dreamt about you a lot . . . my whole life."

"Really?"

"Yeah, I dream a lot."

"Yeah, what about?"

"I dream a lot about a man on a tightrope. Maybe it was Harold working on the skyscrapers. And—"

Jessica's face suddenly went stony. Then she turned and stomped out of the room.

What did I say?

I went into the living room. Gramma and Harold were glued to the TV, watching the news. It was about the Mohawk blockade over in Kanehsatake.

"What's going on?"

"Our brothers and sisters in Kanehsatake won't remove their roadblock."

"It's about the golf course, right?"

"Yes," Harold answered. "The Oka townspeople don't understand that the land is a sacred burial spot."

"This could get ugly," Gramma said.

This is what I was dreaming about. A chill ran down my spine. *Someone's gonna get hurt.*

LATER that day I phoned Dana to tell her about the blockade.

"Wow, that is so cool! Nothing ever happens here. Maybe I'll chop my hair off and dye it green." She laughed. "Just to spice things up."

"Don't you dare."

"How is everything going?"

"My head's spinning. There's all kinds of stuff happening."

We chatted for a bit. Then I went to bed.

> *The white bird is flying in circles.*
> *Its wings are spread wide, soaring.*
> *Then suddenly it explodes, and*
> *feathers float down, piling up at my*
> *feet.*

"CARRIE! Jessica! Ma!" Harold's voice was urgent.

I jumped out of bed and ran into the living room.

"Pack your things and come with me," Harold said.

"What's happening?" Gramma asked.

"The police attacked the blockade in Kanehsatake. We've put up our own roadblocks here in support. There's one right in front of our driveway. We also blocked the Mercier Bridge."

"Oh my God," Jessica said.

"It's better if you three stay with Aunt Clare in town until things calm down. Get ready."

"WARRIORS," Gramma whispered as we pulled out of the driveway.

Men in camouflage stood guard. Their faces were hidden behind bandanas. Some held rifles, others held binoculars.

My dream.

One of the men nodded and waved. He was wearing a dark ball cap with a white bird stitched on the side.

Tommy!

Chapter 12

"Mom!" I shout. "Mom! I need you! Hurry!"
I see Mom run toward me, her medicine kit
in her hand. I'm watching a heart monitor;
it flat-lines. I'm frozen in fear, unsure of
what to do, unsure of how to help. A shrill
ring from the machine startles me into
action. I grab for a drumstick and start
pounding on a motionless body. Every time
I pound it, I hear the rhythmic beat of a
drum and a little blip flashes across the heart
monitor. "Hurry, Mom! Quick!"

I AWOKE TO THE SOUND OF A TV. I HAD FALLEN ASLEEP ON
the couch at Aunt Clare's house. A warrior, his face covered
with a bandana, was on the screen.

Tommy?

Gramma was sitting beside me on the couch. Aunt Clare
was pacing back and forth across the living room rug.

Jessica was biting her nails in front of the TV. "Everyone's talking about that policeman who was shot this morning when they attacked the roadblock."

"Shot and killed," Aunt Clare said. She nervously twisted the rings on her fingers as she talked.

"It's bad," Gramma said. "Very bad."

"Why don't they take the blockades down," I asked, "before one of us gets hurt?"

"They can't take it down because the land they are protecting is a sacred gathering place and burial ground," Gramma said. "It's all about protecting our rights and standing up for ourselves."

"Our Mercier Bridge blockade has stopped the commuters from going to Montreal, and the townspeople are furious," Jessica said, her face set hard. "That will show them we mean business. If the police attack the roadblock again, we'll blow up the bridge."

My stomach knotted, and a lump formed in my throat.

I was on edge for the next three days, watching the television and waiting for some word about Tommy and Harold. Finally Harold walked in with his arm around Tommy's shoulder. "Look who I found!"

I ran over and hugged them both, choking back tears.

Thank God they're all right.

"Tommy, you remember my other daughter, Jessica," Harold said.

Jessica stood up and they shook hands.

"Yeah, you used to hang around the hockey rink, back when your dad was coaching us."

"Jessica was too shy then to talk to the players." Harold ruffled Jessica's hair.

"Stop it, Dad, I'm not a little kid." Jessica shrugged him off.

"Tommy needs a place to crash," Harold said. "He can't get home."

"I'll make up the girls' room for him," Aunt Clare said, heading down the hall. "And you two can sleep in my room."

"Girls, make something for dinner," Gramma added, shooing us into the kitchen.

"Gramma, there's not much food left," Jessica said, rummaging in the cupboard. "Just peanut butter and some old bread."

"I'll go get groceries," I volunteered.

"We just stopped at the store in town," Tommy said. "It was crazy in there. The shelves have been cleaned out."

Jessica dumped the bread and the jar of peanut butter on the table, and we made a bunch of sandwiches.

"I'll see if I can get through to Gramma's house later and pick up some food," Harold said, between bites. "And Carrie, you'd better call your parents and give them an update. Let them know that the roads are blocked, and that there's no way they'll get through. Make sure you tell them you're safe."

"Okay," I said, popping the last bite of sandwich into my mouth.

"Harold, we need to get back to the blockade," said Tommy, standing up and wiping some crumbs off his trousers.

"I'll go along with you," Jessica said.

"It's too dangerous," Tommy said.

"Too much fighting," Harold added.

"Some things are worth fighting for," Jessica said.

"Leave the fighting to us. Let's go, Tommy."

After they left, I called my parents.

"Hi, Mom."

"Hello? Carrie?" Mom sounded anxious. "Oh honey, we've been sick to death with worry. Are you okay? Are you safe?"

"I'm safe," I said. *At least I hope I am.* "We're at Aunt Clare's house."

"We really miss you."

"I miss you both too. A lot." I was surprised to realize that I actually meant it.

I gave them an update about the blockade, but they'd already heard all about it from the news. Then I went to move my things to Aunt Clare's bedroom to make room for Tommy. Jessica was there, dressed in a black turtleneck and tying a bandana around her face. She tugged a black baseball cap down over her eyes.

Jessica put her finger over her lips, opened the window and disappeared into the darkness.

WHEN I got back to the kitchen, Aunt Clare was gripping Gramma's shoulders. "Ma had a little fainting spell."

"I've been a little dizzy lately, honey. Nothing to worry about." She looked really pale.

"You need to see a doctor," I said, concerned.

I wish Mom and Dad were here. They could help.

"I don't need a doctor, Carrie," Gramma said, as Aunt

Clare handed her a mug of tea. "I get my medicine from Mother Earth."

She looks like the sick old woman in my dream.

IT was the next night. Aunt Clare had gone over to Gramma's house with Harold to pick up food. Jessica was at the blockade, and I was snuggled up on the couch with Tommy. Gramma was asleep—she'd been sleeping all day. I watched her chest rise and fall with each breath. *God, I hope she's alright.*

Tommy tucked my hair behind my ear. "I need your help filming. I'm doing a story on the blockade."

"I don't know anything about cameras."

"All you need to do is hold the camera steady and press a button. It's easy."

"But it's dangerous at the blockade."

"You'll be with me. Everything will be fine."

"I don't know." I hesitated.

"Pleeeease, Carrie," he drawled, lowering his head so that his lips were just inches from my neck. "I'd really appreciate your help."

Goosebumps popped up all along my arms. "Okay," I said.

Just then I heard a car pull into the driveway. I jumped up and went to open the front door. Harold and Aunt Clare were trudging up the path, each carrying two grocery bags. "This is from Gramma's," Harold said. "It's all there is left."

I followed them into the kitchen. Tommy came in after me.

"Police have blocked all deliveries," Aunt Clare said, "even food and medicine. We'll have to ration this food."

"I don't know how long it will last," Harold added. "We have to go out again. We'll be back in a bit."

"So how about helping me with the story?" Tommy said after Harold and Aunt Clare left.

"I'll go get ready," I said.

I wound my hair into a tight braid that fell down my back. Tommy gave me a Blackhawks cap, a camouflage bandana and a pair of black steel-toed work boots. The heavy soles made me a full two inches taller.

We set out in Tommy's car, and a few minutes later we were at the roadblock. We parked and Tommy handed me the video recorder.

Dozens of men dressed in fatigues were walking back and forth on our side of the blockade. Some had weapons—shotguns, handguns, knives.

I started filming.

Fists waved through the air, people shouted, rocks and flaming bottles flew everywhere.

"I'm ready," Tommy said, straightening his shoulders. "You're on."

"Tensions rise at the roadblock on Route 138 in Kahnawake. The situation is volatile. The Mohawk Nation is defending its rights and culture. We stand strong with our brothers and sisters in Kanehsatake. We won't fire unless fired upon. We will not take the first shot. But if we are attacked, we are prepared to fight . . . even die."

Just then a flaming bottle flipped through the air, smashed into the ground and exploded near where Tommy stood.

He jumped out of the way and grabbed me, pulling me away from the flames. "That's enough for tonight. Let's get you out of here."

I need to warn him. He's in danger.

"Listen," I said, as I walked beside him toward the car, "what happened there, with the bottle exploding, is just like the dream I've been having over and over. You're in danger."

"Carrie, we're all in danger."

Chapter 13

A steady drumbeat. The man with a long braid, wearing a ball cap, navy turtleneck and jeans is standing atop a pile of tires. He raises his rifle. He turns toward me. A bandana covers his face and the cap covers his eyes. Suddenly a fireball hits him, and he bursts into flames. He shoots his rifle and topples from the tire pile. A patter of gunfire follows. A white bird lies dead at my feet, blood dripping from its neck.

ANOTHER COUPLE OF DAYS HAD PASSED.

I'm never going back to the roadblock. I shivered as I recalled the night when I went there with Tommy. It was just like my dreams.

"CARRIE! The phone's for you. It's your mom," Gramma shouted, waking me up.

I hopped out of bed, shuffled into the kitchen in my PJs and took the phone from Gramma. "Hi, Mom."

"Honey, I've cancelled all my appointments and I'm driving up."

"There's a roadblock. I can't get out and you can't get in."

"I know, but I want to be close by you."

"We're worried," Dad broke in. He was on the other phone.

"I'm safe here at Aunt Clare's, Dad."

"Your mom and I have been watching the news. It looks pretty scary there."

My calm quiet life in McDonalds Corners felt like a lifetime ago.

"Dad has surgery scheduled, but I'm leaving first thing tomorrow morning. We love you so much."

"I love you too."

TOMMY, Jessica and I were sitting around the kitchen table. Gramma pulled a bag of oatmeal out from under the sink. She dished two spoonfuls into each of our bowls and poured hot water over the oatmeal. There was hardly enough for breakfast. The food that Harold and Aunt Clare had brought from Gramma's was nearly gone.

"Aren't you having anything to eat, Gramma?" I asked.

"I don't have much of an appetite right now."

She's barely eating anything now. She puts lots of food on my plate and Jessica's plate, but hardly any on her own.

Just then we heard wheels screeching on gravel, a car door slam shut and footsteps in the hallway. Aunt Clare came rushing into the kitchen. "It's Aunt Becky. She's been hurt."

"What?" Gramma cried.

"She was trying to get through the roadblock. The police told her to turn around. There were lots of other cars full of kids and old people."

Gramma sat down and sighed heavily.

"How'd she get hurt?" Tommy asked.

"A mob surrounded her car," said Aunt Clare. "She had her boys with her."

"Those bastards," Jessica growled.

"They smashed the windshield with bats, and the glass shattered in her face. The boys are okay, though."

"Is she hurt bad?" I asked.

"She's pretty shaken up, and her face is a mess. I'll stay with her for a few nights to keep an eye on her and help take care of the boys," Aunt Clare said. She gave Gramma a kiss and turned to leave.

"Oh my poor Becky," Gramma said, as the front door slammed shut. "She should have waited for the supplies."

"Supplies?" Jessica asked.

"I talked to your father this morning. He and some others rowed across the river to the Dorval side to pick up food and medicine."

"The Dorval side?" Tommy asked.

"Yes, some friends from Kahnawake crossed before the Chateauguay blockade went up. You three better go over to the seaway to meet them."

SOON we were at the seaway, about half a mile away from the Mercier Bridge. A few people from the reserve were milling around, waiting.

A motorboat was slowly chugging its way toward us. Harold was leaning against one of the other men in the boat, his shirt stained with blood.

"Dad, what happened?" Jessica cried as the boat beached.

"A mob attacked us with baseball bats," he said, as Tommy helped him out of the boat. "They cornered me. My leg's really bad."

"Are you okay?" I asked.

"I don't think it's broken, but they threw all our supplies into the river—everything."

We helped Harold hobble over to the car.

"I hate them," Jessica said.

"Don't hold hatred in your heart, Jessica," Harold said. "It'll destroy you. Carrie, help me into the car."

"Sure, Dad," I said. Realizing I called him "Dad" for the first time, my heart skipped a beat.

Is there room in my life for two dads?

Harold put his arm around my shoulders, and I slowly lowered him onto the passenger seat. He winced and closed his eyes.

WHEN we got back, Tommy helped Harold to his bed. Then the phone rang. Jessica answered it.

"It's your mom, Carrie," she said, handing it to me.

"Hi, honey."

"Hi, Mom. Where are you?"

"I was at the roadblock. I couldn't get through. Are you okay?"

"I'm fine."

"Stay away from that mess over there—it's dangerous."

"Don't worry, Mom."

"I'm staying at the Sundown Hotel in Chateauguay."

I wrote down the phone number.

"Call me back really soon, sweetie. I need to know you're okay."

"I will."

I went to Harold's room to check on him. He was sitting up, so I went in and hugged him.

"How're you doing?" he asked.

"I was so scared," I said. "More to the point, how are you doing?"

"I'll be fine. Everything is going to be okay," he said, "as long as you and your sister are safe."

"I wasn't scared for me, I was scared for you. I don't want anything to happen to you. We've just found each other."

His body stiffened; he took in a deep breath and held it. I thought he was trying to stop himself from crying. "I'll be more careful," he finally said. "I promise."

"I wish you didn't have to go back there," I said.

"I know," he said, "but I have to."

"I understand." I wiped a tear from my cheek with the back of my hand.

"I know you do, Carrie. You're my daughter."

"I've been talking to Gramma and Tommy a lot. I know how important it is to stand up for our people," I said.

Our people . . . I'm where I belong.

"Carrie, you don't know how happy I am that I've found you. My life is complete now. Our story is only just beginning."

I leaned over and hugged him. *My dad!*

I got him a drink of water and pulled the blankets back up over his shoulders, then went into the kitchen to check on Gramma. She was holding on to Jessica. "Gramma's feeling faint," Jessica said.

"Let's get her to the couch," I said.

Jessica and I helped Gramma into the living room and lowered her onto the couch.

I wrapped a blanket around her shoulders. "Best that you lie down, Gramma."

She nodded, swung her feet up, closed her eyes and fell asleep.

Jessica and I sat beside each other in silence, watching Gramma sleep.

After a few minutes, I looked over at Jessica. "Why did you run away?"

"Because."

"Because why?" I prodded.

She stared at me, and I thought she was going to get up and leave.

"Because of my dreams," she said.

"Your dreams?" I asked.

"My dreams told me I had to leave. I didn't want to go, but I had to."

"Where did you go?" I asked.

"Most of the time I just hid out in the forest. I know the woods like the back of my hand." She smiled. "Sometimes I just wish . . ." She paused.

"Wish what?" I pressed.

"Oh never mind. I don't want to talk about it." She got up and stormed out.

Gramma was still sleeping, so I pulled out my dream journal and started doodling. When I stopped drawing, the pages were covered with birds. One sat on Tommy's shoulder; one perched atop Jessica's head. Another was half bird, half woman.

Startled, I dropped the book.

"She'll come around, Carrie," Gramma said, opening her eyes. "Don't worry."

I stood and helped her sit up, then sat back down beside her.

"You have our gift," Gramma said. "Your dreams."

I didn't say anything.

"You see things."

"You have dreams too, Gramma?"

"Yes. So did my mother. So did my grandmother. So does Jessica." She took my hands and looked into my eyes. "Your dreams are powerful, Carrie. Your dreams tell you who you are truly meant to be. They are a gift from your ancestors. Learn to understand them. They hold the answers you are seeking."

"There is always a drumming sound in my dreams. What does that mean?"

"Drumming is very important to us. It's a form of prayer, a form of celebration, an acknowledgement of our ancestors and the good things the Creator has given us."

"And I keep dreaming about a white bird too."

"Ahh, that's no ordinary bird. It's a white eagle. It's your spirit guide. My spirit guide is a white eagle too."

"My spirit guide?"

"It watches over you. It shows you your true destiny."

I wrapped my arms around Gramma and cried. Her words felt so right. *Finally, someone I can talk to. Someone who understands me.* I kissed her cheek.

Just then Tommy walked in. "I'm heading back to the blockade. Do you want to come along?"

"Okay."

As Tommy and I drove to the roadblock, a tiny white light flickered deep in the forest. I was afraid, but I had to figure out what my dreams meant. I had to be brave.

We pulled up and parked.

"I need to talk to you about something," Tommy said.

"Oh my God!" I interrupted, grabbing the camera and jumping out of the car.

The crowd on the Chateauguay side of the roadblock was in full riot. Rocks and bricks flew through the air. Police fired tear gas and strode into the crowd with their batons.

I fixed the camera on a large burning figure.

"They're burning effigies," Tommy said.

A group of Mohawk men sat in a circle around a large drum, drumming. I took a step back to get a better camera angle.

The drumming in my dreams! My heartbeat quickened to match the drums. Each stroke of a drumstick sent a burst of energy racing through me.

All of a sudden there was a loud explosion behind me.

I turned around and saw Jessica. She had her turtleneck pulled up over her nose, and a ball cap pulled down low over her eyes. The drumbeat grew louder and louder. I turned in time to see a white light flash behind the drum circle.

My spirit guide! It's a warning!

I turned again to look for Jessica, but she had disappeared.

Chapter 14

I pull a needle from my first-aid kit, flick the tip and kneel beside the unconscious woman. The white eagle dances to the rhythm of the drums in the clear blue sky just above us. I plunge the needle into her arm, and she opens her eyes, coming back to life. I have healed her.

I WOKE UP FROM THE DREAM IN A COLD SWEAT.

I went to the kitchen to find Gramma staring at a bowl of oatmeal. "Gramma, are you feeling okay?"

"I'm fine," she answered, listlessly.

She had a bandage on her hand. "What happened to your hand?"

"It's nothing," she said. "Didn't I tell you? I cut myself with a paring knife, peeling apples."

"But that was back when we were still at your house. It hasn't stopped bleeding yet?"

I reached for her hand.

"No, it hasn't healed," Gramma said, looking at her hand. Then she swayed and slid sideways onto the linoleum floor. I knelt beside her.

"Gramma, wake up!"

She didn't respond.

"Help!" I shouted.

Silence.

Oh God! We're all alone.

I phoned Aunt Clare at Becky's. No answer. "Aunt Clare! Come home! It's Gramma, she needs you!" I shouted into the answering machine.

I remembered my dreams. Mom rushing to help me. Flatline. Me bringing someone back to life with a needle.

I put my fingers against her neck.

Heart attack? No, she still has a pulse. Ongoing condition? No, she doesn't go to a doctor; she doesn't take medicine. She is always thirsty, always drinking her tea. She walks through the forest every day for exercise. She has blurry vision—has to strain to read the labels when baking. She has a cut that won't heal. That's it—diabetes! She needs insulin.

I grabbed the phone and called Mom at the hotel.

"Gramma fainted!" I shouted. "She must have diabetes, she needs insulin!"

"Is she breathing?"

"Just a minute." I leaned over Gramma and saw her chest rise and fall.

"Yes, she's breathing."

"Is there a doctor on the reserve?"

"I don't know. Mom, I need your help! Now!"

' "How can I get there? How can I get through the blockade?"
The phone went dead. *What do I do now?*

JESSICA finally came home. When she saw Gramma, she knelt beside her and placed an ear over her heart.

"We need to get my mom here, past the roadblock."

"No way, we can't leave Gramma alone," Jessica said.

"It's the only way," I said, pulling Jessica's arm with one hand and grabbing the car keys from the table with the other. "Aunt Clare will be home soon."

"Do you even know how to drive?" Jessica asked, pulling the seatbelt over her shoulder.

"I've got my learner's," I said, hopping into the driver's seat. I put it in reverse and stepped on the gas. The car jolted backward. I slammed hard on the brakes, put it in drive and took off. "Can you get us through the roadblock?"

"Yes," she said, "there's a path through the forest."

A few minutes later Jessica said, "Stop here."

I pulled the car over. We were at least half a mile away from the roadblock. I could see the warriors in the distance. A flame flew through the air and exploded when it hit the ground. Jessica and I both shuddered.

"This way," Jessica said, leading me toward the forest. I ran quickly behind her. We jumped over wide puddles that zigzagged through the field until we came to the edge of the woods.

"Here we go," she said, pulling a branch aside and jumping in. It was dark. My legs burned. A knot in my stomach grew tighter and tighter.

I hope she knows where she's going.

I ran, arms raised to protect my face, but branches hit and scratched me as we raced through the squelching mud. I saw a white bird off in the distance. *My spirit guide.*

Jessica slowed and pointed. "We're here. Your mom's hotel is just over there," she whispered. "Coast is clear."

"I'll be right back." I took off, out of the safety and protection of the forest.

"Mom!" I called, running toward her. She was standing under a street lamp in front of the hotel, waiting.

"Carrie!" she shouted, wrapping her arms around me. "Are you okay?"

"I'm fine. You have the insulin?"

Mom patted her backpack and nodded. "Let's go."

I grabbed her hand and we turned to run. We stopped when we saw a crowd of people gathered in front of the spot where I had left the forest. *We're blocked!* I could see the flaming figure of a burning Mohawk effigy flying through the air at the site of the roadblock. *Maybe that's what they'll do to me if they catch me.*

I tugged Mom's arm. "We'll find another way." I led her away from the crowd.

"Psst," Jessica hissed. I could see her in the dark woods,

waving her arms at us. There was a faint white light above her. Turning quickly to make sure no one was watching us, we slipped into the woods.

I hope we're not too late!

AUNT Clare was sitting next to Gramma when we returned. Gramma was still on the floor, but Aunt Clare had tucked a pillow under her head and had draped a blanket over her.

My mom pulled her medical kit out of her backpack. "Good thing your mother's a doctor," Aunt Clare said.

We stood back while Mom examined Gramma, peppering us with questions.

She took out a hypodermic needle and a small vial. "You're right, she's in diabetic shock. It's a good thing you told me to bring insulin."

She swabbed her upper arm and jabbed her with the needle. "Thank goodness we're on time. People die from this a lot."

Mom stood up and lifted Gramma from under her arms. "Clare, help me get her onto the couch. I'll rig up an IV drip for her."

With Gramma settled comfortably on the couch, Aunt Clare turned on the TV for an update.

I dropped into the chair, exhausted. *My dream saved Gramma!*

"The army is moving in," the television reporter shouted. "One shot from either side could cause the situation in Kahnawake to erupt in a bloodbath!"

Chapter 15

I am looking in the mirror. A long black braid snakes over my shoulder, and I'm wearing a bandana and a black baseball cap. A gunshot cracks, and my braid bursts into flames. Blood pours out from my eyes—but the eyes are not mine. A white eagle lies dead at my feet. Loud drumming beats in the background.

I WOKE UP AND RUSHED INTO THE LIVING ROOM TO SEE how Gramma was doing. "How are you feeling, Gramma?"

She was sitting up on the couch, knitting, but still looked a little pale.

"I feel pretty good. Your mom is taking great care of me."

I sat with Gramma all day to keep an eye on her. Later that night, Mom spoke to Dad on the telephone. "The news report says the army will be moving in very soon. They say it could end up in a bloodbath."

I caught a glimpse of Jessica sneaking down the hallway. She was wearing jeans, a blue turtleneck and a black baseball cap. She stopped to look in the mirror before she headed toward the door.

I suddenly understood.

Then I heard the front door click shut.

"Gramma . . ." I began, but she held up her hand. Her eyes bored into me, and my heart skipped a beat.

"It's up to you now," she said in a quiet voice.

I nodded.

AT the roadblock, I couldn't see Jessica anywhere. A bunch of warriors in camouflage moved en masse across the field. Tommy stood next to a very old warrior with long white braids who was sitting on a blanket, drumming. Tommy was pointing his camera toward the blockade.

The drumbeat grew louder and louder.

"Tommy!" I shouted, waving. "Tommy!"

I ran up to him, breathless.

"Carrie! Quick," he said, handing me the camera. "You film! This is big stuff!"

I held up my hand. "No, Tommy. Jessica—have you seen her? This is important."

"What? No, I haven't. I have to get this on film. There are tanks over there!"

But I wasn't listening to Tommy. Across the clearing, a young warrior was handing someone a rifle. *Jessica!*

"Jessica! Jessica!" I shouted. But over the drumming and bottle rockets and tanks rumbling in the distance, she couldn't hear me. The crowd jostled me back and forth, and I lost sight of her.

A white flash caught my eye. There she was, on top of a pile of tires at the front of the blockade. The air around us was bright with the flare of bottle rockets.

Jessica raised her rifle in the air and shouted, pumping her fist. Her long braid swung from side to side.

I ran toward the tire pile as fast as I could through the crowd of warriors, climbed up and grabbed her arm. "Jessica, put down the gun!"

Jessica pushed me away. "Back off, Carrie."

I windmilled my arms to regain my balance. "My dream! You're going to get shot!"

"Screw your dream," Jessica cried, raising the rifle high above her head.

Just then a small rock hit me on the forehead, right above my eye. Warm blood trickled down my cheek.

"Jessica, please . . . trust me."

Suddenly there were shouts.

"Duck!"

"Watch out!"

"Move away!"

A bottle rocket was flying right at Jessica.

I grabbed the handle of her rifle and yanked her out of the way. She toppled down the pile of tires. A loud explosion. A searing pain in my hip. My arm was on fire.

I dropped from the tire pile and rolled frantically in the dirt, trying to extinguish the flames.

Something soft fell on top of me. It was a blanket. Tommy knelt beside me and rolled me back and forth to put out the flames. Then he scooped me up into his arms. I nestled my head against his chest, and the world went black.

WHEN I woke up I was in bed, and Jessica was holding my hand.

"You saved my life," she said. "You stopped me from making a huge mistake. I've been unfair to you."

I squeezed her hand.

"I finally realized what I've been looking for," Jessica said. "You. You are what I've been missing. Sometimes you don't see what's right in front of you."

"Maybe I could have tried harder to find out where I belong."

"I was angry at you."

"Why?"

"When I was still in foster care, I used to dream about another life. A family who loved me, a nice house, a big bedroom with lots of toys to play with. I thought it was me I was dreaming about; the life I was meant to have growing up. Even after our dad found me, I kept having those dreams—I still felt like something was missing from my life. Now I realize that my dreams were telling me where you were, and that it was you that was missing from my life."

"But you have that now—a family who loves you."

"Yes," she said, "and now I have a sister."

"Why did you keep running away?"

"When I first came here, I felt special. Gramma told me about her dreams. She told me I had the same gift. But soon after I arrived, my dreams started telling me I had to leave.

I tried to ignore them, but they wouldn't stop. I had to listen to them; I had to leave. When I learned you were found because of the missing person poster from the last time I ran away, I finally understood what my dreams meant. But when you came here, I felt I wasn't special anymore. It seemed to me that everyone just cared about you."

"Yes, I understand now. It must have been hard."

"It felt like when I was back in the foster homes. In each new home, everyone paid lots of attention to me, until a new kid came. Then they forgot about me until I got shuffled off to the next foster home."

"There's plenty of love for both of us."

And I can love two families, two dads.

She leaned over, hugged me and left the room.

"How are you feeling?" Gramma asked, walking in.

"I'm okay," I said.

"You saved a lot of people. If Jessica had fired that gun, I can't imagine what would have happened."

"You knew?"

"I have dreams too, remember? You and Jessica had to find a way to come together. When you saved her life, she understood your love."

"Did your dreams tell you about me?"

"Yes. I knew Jessica would bring you to us." She patted me on the shoulder, kissed my cheek and left.

Tommy walked in a few minutes later. "Things have calmed down a little at the blockade. Guess what?"

"What?"

"I talked to my mom this morning. I've just been accepted into Ryerson for journalism." He beamed.

"Wow! That's amazing!" I said. "That's in Toronto, right?"

I realized I might not see him again. It was a long way from McDonalds Corners.

"Don't worry, Carrie. We'll figure it out. You're stuck with me. There's something about you, your energy. It draws me to you. It has since the moment I met you. I tried to tell you, but I didn't want to freak you out."

He leaned over and kissed me on the lips.

"Okay, time for rest," Mom called from the doorway. She had her arms crossed, but she was smiling.

THREE weeks later, Harold came in, relief washed over his face. "Early this morning, a group of warriors laid a peace pipe before the army officers. They talked and shook hands. It's over."

We all cheered.

We moved our stuff back to Gramma's house that morning.

I was sitting on the porch with Jessica after lunch. Mom and Gramma were coming out of the forest. Mom carried a little straw basket, brimming with leaves, berries and twigs.

"Hi, girls," they said as they went into the house.

I smiled at them.

AFTER being closed for fifty-eight days, the Mercier Bridge was finally reopened. Dad and Dana came to pick us up. We packed up the car and said our goodbyes. Then we all hugged—a big, group bear hug.

Kahnawake or McDonalds Corners, it doesn't matter. As long as I have the love of my family, my entire family, I will always be exactly where I belong.

I saw a white eagle swoop toward us and spread its wings. I felt the group hug get tighter, and I imagined the eagle wrapping its wings around us, bringing my two families together.

We waved goodbye as we began to pull out.

"Wait!" Jessica shouted, running toward the car.

Dad stopped the car and I opened my window.

"Close your eyes," she said.

I did, and she placed something bulky on my lap.

"I made this for you."

I opened my eyes. It was a drum. Its sides were stitched with exquisite beadwork. The centre of the drum was painted with a picture of two girls—each a mirror of the other—dancing beneath the wings of a white eagle.

They were holding hands.